StreetSmarts

How Life's Hustlers Taught Me to Sell

Based on True Events

- A note from author -

Whether you're in sales or just love a good story, this book offers a candid look at the grind, grit, and humor that make up the world of selling.

You can expect a witty, behind-the-scenes journey into the real world of sales—far from the polished, motivational speeches.

This book brings to life the raw, entertaining, and often hilarious struggles of salespeople as they navigate the highs and lows of closing deals, meeting quotas, and handling impossible clients.

It's filled with practical insights, secrets of the trade, and stories of triumph and failure that are relatable, engaging, and refreshingly honest.

Preface

This book is dedicated to the unsung heroes of the sales fraternity—those who turn relentless hustle into success, and tackle targets with a mix of grit and wit. To those who turn coffee into cash, face rejection with a smile, and navigate the daily grind with unyielding determination: this one's for you.

These stories are inspired by real events, but don't expect a self-help guide. Instead, brace yourself for a rollicking ride through office chaos, romance, sales mishaps and the quirky characters who make the world of sales so wildly entertaining. Buckle up, laugh hard, and remember: in sales, humor and brotherhood are the best survival strategies!

Whether you're in sales or just love a good story, this book offers a candid look at the grind, grit, and humor that make up the world of selling. You can expect a witty, behind-the-scenes journey into the real world of sales—far from the polished, motivational speeches.

This book brings to life the raw, entertaining, and often hilarious struggles of salespeople as they navigate the highs and lows of closing deals, meeting quotas, and handling impossible clients. It's filled with practical insights, secrets of the trade, and stories of triumph and failure that are relatable, engaging, and refreshingly honest.

Dedication

This book is dedicated to the unsung heroes of the sales fraternity—those who turn relentless hustle into success and tackle targets with a mix of grit and wit. To those who turn coffee into cash, face rejection with a smile, and navigate the daily grind with unyielding determination: this one's for you.

I would like to extend my heartfelt thanks to my family and friends, who have been my constant support. To my sister, Radhika, and my brother, Akash, your unwavering encouragement and belief in me have been invaluable. To my son, Akshat, your boundless energy and joy inspire me every day.

A special and loving tribute goes to my dear friend Dolas, who is no longer with us. Your camaraderie, spirit, and friendship are deeply missed, and this book is a testament to the impact you made on my life.

With gratitude and affection,
Deepak Dubey

The Learnings

Morning Mayhem: The Office Drama Chronicles"

Tandon always waltzed in at 8:30 AM, though the official start time was 9 AM. I think he enjoyed watching the rest of us get chewed out while he sipped his coffee with a smirk.

Enter Dolas, the self-proclaimed Salman Khan fanboy. Tight jeans, tighter shirt, the whole gym-bro ensemble. Just as he's strutting to the washroom, Venky's voice booms, "Dolas! Why are you late again? It's 9:05! Fix this!"

"Yes, boss," Dolas muttered, his swagger momentarily deflated.

Two minutes later, in strolls Jain, the MBA from London on his first job. He arrives in a luxury Honda City, both courtesy of his doting father. One hand gripping a coffee mug, the other juggling a jacket, earphones blasting hard rock, and dancing to his own beat like he's already nailed his sales target.

Venky's face lit up with a predatory grin. "Jain! JAIN! Over here, now!"

Jain, in his own world, had to be nudged by a colleague to snap to attention. "Yes, Venky? What's up?"

"Why are you late again? Enjoy your coffee, are we? Want a refill?"

"Sorry, boss, won't happen again," Jain replied, barely suppressing a grin.

"That's the third time this week! Should I believe you?" Venky fumed.

"Boss, I am a little late, and drinking coffee but if you peeked at the stairs, you'd see what others are up to. I'm not the only one breaking rules, at least I walked inside the office"

Jain had a knack for throwing everyone else under the bus, earning him the nickname sabkibajao.com.

Venky practically flew down the stairs, crossing two doors and a floor in record time. He found Kadu, Poojary, and the freshers, all puffing away. "You three, my office, now! You have zero respect! And you, newbie, stay away from these bad influences!"

The morning drama was like a live-action soap opera. Jain, meanwhile, sat back, enjoying the show, knowing he'd escaped Venky's wrath yet again

---

Tandon: The Early Bird with a Secret'

Tandon was the early bird who got the worm—or in his case, the pleasure of watching others get roasted by Venky. Officially due by 9 AM, Tandon always strolled in at 8:30, just early enough to chuckle at everyone else's misfortunes.

By 9:30, Tandon would ceremoniously shut down his desktop, even though he lugged his laptop to work every day. Why he needed both was a mystery, but who was I to question his rituals?

We both lived in Mira Road and worked in Andheri, so we commuted together. Little did Venky know, I waited outside Tandon's place for a good 10-15 minutes every day, making Tandon look like the punctual hero.

Our Andheri office was a stylish oasis amid Mumbai's chaotic traffic. Inside, it was all sleek floors, fancy coffee machines, and senior managers lounging in plush, oversized cabins. The dress code? Think runway-ready. Colleagues strutted around in designer outfits, flashing the latest gadgets like trophies. Sales stars carried phones fancier than their titles, with enough cologne in the air to make you wonder if you'd accidentally walked into a perfume shop. If your clothes and gadgets didn't scream "I'm successful," were you even working here?

One day, as Tandon was about to leave the office, I called out, "Hey, mind if I join you for your meetings? Got nothing lined up today, and Venky's not gonna be thrilled seeing me here after 11 AM."

He hesitated, "No friend, I usually prefer flying solo on meetings. You should focus on booking your own."

But after some persuasion, he reluctantly agreed. However, none of his so-called clients were available. "Let's just sit somewhere and make calls," he suggested.

I figured we'd go to a café or something. Nope. Back to his place in Mira Road. His bachelor pad screamed "I live alone": leftover pizza, dusty pans, and newspapers everywhere. He was quite the unexpected reader.

"I need to be in a good mood to make calls," I thought. Meanwhile, Tandon said, "I'm gonna have cornflakes and take a nap. Menu cards are in the drawer if you want to order."

Next to the table were a couple of magazines featuring scantily clad women, with many pages mysteriously glued together. Clearly, Ayush had been indulging in some "private reading" sessions and playing with his "little brother" Baburao when he thought no one was watching.

It was 1 PM. "This jerk isn't even offering me lunch on my first visit," I fumed silently. But I ordered Chinese rice and cold drinks, got into the zone, and started calling clients.

Tandon woke up at 4 PM, fresh as a daisy, and began making calls with a pitch that could sell sand in the desert. "Hi, Sudhir, Tandon here from Jobs.Com. Can we chat about how we can help with your recruitment needs?"

He secured four appointments in no time. If he made 100 calls, he'd probably secure 40. I was floored.

Venky's call interrupted our hustle. Tandon's phone had this nifty feature that played ambient sounds during calls. "Yes, Venky, I'm outside the client's office, traffic's a killer. Can I call you back?"

Venky bought it. Every. Single. Time.

"Let's get back to the office," Tandon snapped.

Curious, I asked, "How many meetings do you do in a week?"

"Three to four. I pick clients who have money and a need. No point creating needs like other salespeople."

Tandon returned to the office at 6 PM, filed his reports, and left by 6:30 PM sharp. Back to Mira Road.

Lazy or genius? Tandon closed enough deals to hit 70-80% of his targets without breaking a sweat. And that Chinese phone with surround sound recording? I needed one stat. Not that I could lie as smoothly as Tandon, but it was worth a shot.

His routine—commute, power nap, **killer sales pitch**—was a daily **masterpiece of efficiency**

"Poojary: The Spoiler/Entertainer"

Picture this: three rebels caught red-handed, puffing away on the office stairs, with Poojary leading the pack. Hailing from Thane, the City of Lakes, a district adjacent to Mumbai, this guy's a linguistic powerhouse, juggling Marathi, English, and Hindi like a pro. Always pacing around the office, dialing up potential clients with the volume turned up to 11—just loud enough for Venky to hear and maybe, just maybe, cut him some slack on those targets.

Reluctantly, Poojary became the "mentor" for the new recruits. "Come with me, I'm your chauffeur today," he announced, striding towards me with a grin that screamed, "Welcome to the jungle!"

"You're my chauffeur? What do you mean by that?" I asked, bewildered.

"You need an explanation now, you dumbfuck? I've got a vehicle and I'm training you on sales meetings today."

Every day, Poojary rode his bike from Thane City, grumbling about how outsiders were the root of all Mumbai's problems, from traffic jams to general chaos. Ironically, as an outsider myself, I quietly nodded along, wondering why he hadn't yet joined a political party.

Poojary was a foodie, a common ground we shared. Before hitting our appointments, he dragged me to a seafood joint near Andheri station. Two fish thalis (Bombil & Tisrya), rice, and chicken gravy later, I was hooked. "Bhai, if we're gonna face Venky's wrath, let's at least be well-fed. Beer?" he asked, conspiratorially. Who was I to refuse? Heaven, if it exists, better have this on the menu.

"Are we ordering anything else? We do have calls, right?" I asked, fighting off a food coma.

"Nahi yaar, waiting for a friend. Then we go," Poojary said, checking his watch like a man with a plan. Enter Dolas, the sales champ.

"Meet Dolas, the star of our team. Maybe you'll join us if you're lucky," Poojary said. My excitement was through the roof; learning from these guys was going to be an adventure.

After lunch, Poojary asked Dolas, "Got the tickets?"

"No worries, it's Monday afternoon. We'll get in," Dolas replied. I was lost—train tickets?

But we ended up at Sona Cinema, a place I'd passed a million times without noticing. My inner angel screamed, "Say no! You've already had beer!" But the devil on my shoulder whispered, "It's too hot to go anywhere else. Let's have a movie time, and you can take a nap, if you feel like"

The next three days were a blur of appointments and hard lessons. No more daily beers—Poojary and I had jobs to keep. His sales skills were top-notch, but his negotiation tactics? Hilariously bad. He'd whip out the rate card and offer a 20% discount, even though we were only allowed to give 15%.

"Sir, after a 20% discount, this is the final amount," he'd say. Worked like a charm on regular clients, but not on the savvy Gujarati or Marwari ones.

"I'll only settle for a 50% discount," one client demanded.

Poojary, practically on the verge of tears, pleaded, "Sir, please, I have kids. My daughter's school admission is at stake. Please understand my situation."

The client, finally relenting, settled for a 30% discount. I was baffled—why not start lower and negotiate to the allowed 15%?

Cheque in hand, we left the office. "Poojary bhai, Venky will never approve a 30% discount," I warned.

He laughed, "Don't worry, I've got it covered." He pulled out a piece of paper—the rate card. "The one I gave him isn't the original. It's inflated by 20%. Let's head back before Venky calls."

Lesson learned: the guy who seals the deal wins, but ethics? Well, let's hope the client never gets their hands on the original rate card.

Luthra: The Best Sales Guy and Negotiation Ninja

Every morning, Luthra would stroll into the office, head straight for the washroom, and emerge smelling like he bathed in a vat of cologne. He was the most charismatic salesperson you'd ever meet and, unsurprisingly, the top performer in our unit.

I was curious about his secret sauce. Determined to crack the code, I began observing his routine. After his fragrant transformation, he'd sit at his desk with a piece of paper and start jotting down names and phone numbers from a diary he guarded more fiercely than his girlfriend. Then he'd start making calls, always at his desk, unlike Poojary, who roamed the office like a lost puppy while talking.

Luthra would spend about an hour setting up meetings, and his team mirrored his every move. They all sounded the same on their calls—same laugh, same pitch, same greetings. It was like Luthra had cloned himself three times in three different names. They even walked like him, bathed in fragrance, sipped coffee, made lists, and fixed appointments.

These guys were a mystery. They never discussed their meetings or clients with anyone. Even Venky, our boss, was clueless about their whereabouts after the first hour in the office. When they did reappear, they were either logging purchase orders or jamming to tunes on their iPods. Unlike the rest of us, who looked like we shopped at the local flea market, these guys flaunted iPods, expensive phones, and designer clothes. They gave us serious inferiority complexes, like SOBO (South Bombay) kids mingling with slum dwellers.

One day, after relentless pestering, Luthra finally took me along to one of his appointments. I was doing well enough with my targets, but I figured learning from the master couldn't hurt. Luthra had a meeting at an industrial complex in the Mumbai suburbs, and we took an auto-rickshaw. Only Luthra could afford an auto both ways; the rest of us usually took the bus or walked.

Luthra had this quirky habit of asking everyone for directions, knowing most would give him the wrong ones. "Majority wins," he said. "Out of five people, I follow what three tell me. Saves time." He explained that a lot of time is wasted finding parking or the right address, so he preferred autos despite owning a car.

We arrived at the client's office. Luthra wasted no time.

"What price are you expecting for this product?" he asked.

"I'm not sure we need it. We can discuss the price later."

"Okay, no problem. How many CVs do you need to search in our database daily?"

"About 50-60," the client replied.

"I promise that can be met," Luthra assured him. "Now, what price are you seeking?"

"We can't pay much. How about 50% of what we pay your competition?"

"Sir, they'll charge you 20% extra on renewal. You'll end up paying more. If you buy my product for two years, I'll give you a 20% discount. You'll save 60% compared to your current plan."

Deal closed.

In just 10-15 minutes, he secured a two-year deal with advance payment. It was like watching Roger Federer play against a kid from the local playground—the client had no choice but to surrender.

We went to three more meetings that day, and he closed two more deals. Luthra closed in a day what some of our salespeople struggled to close in a month.

It was a masterclass in sales—find your strength and ride it all the way to the bank. For Luthra it was negotiation..hardcore.

"Dolas: Fake It Till You Make It' Masterclass"

Dolas, practically strutted everyday into the office like he was auditioning for a Bollywood movie. Coming straight from South Bombay, Dolas would often drop the line about being a distant relative of Maya Dolas, the infamous gangster from "Shootout at Lokhandwala." I mean, if that didn't add some serious street cred, what would?

Dolas was a Salman Khan fanatic. No, I'm not talking about casual admiration. I'm talking full-on fanboy mode. He'd walk around the office mimicking Salman's iconic dance moves and dropping dialogues like he was auditioning for a role in a sequel. I swear, his love for Salman Khan was so intense that it almost felt like his entire personality was on loan from a Bollywood script.

Now, the first time I saw Dolas, he was squeezing into an auto rickshaw at Andheri station. Picture this: Dolas, drenched in sweat, in a tight shirt that seemed like it might explode from his bulging muscles. I thought, "Dude, maybe let your clothes breathe a bit!" But hey, fashion advice wasn't exactly my forte.

"Dolas, can I join you?" I shouted, trying to catch up with him.We both were at Andheri station, planning to reach office on time.

He turned around with a grin that could light up a room and said, "Sharing is caring, bro. Hop in, we're late!"

He asked the auto driver if he'd go to Kurla station. I was puzzled, like, "Why Kurla?" But Dolas had this look of pure mischief in his eyes. "Don't worry, our office is on the way. I'll drop you off first."

Halfway through the journey, Venky rang Dolas, and Dolas confidently assured him, "Sure thing, boss, I'll be at the office first." But as soon as we hit the office, Dolas turned to the driver and said, "Change of plans, Bhaiyaa. What's the bill?" The driver's face was a masterpiece of confusion and crushed expectations. I couldn't help but chuckle—I knew it wasn't Venky who called him. The whole thing was as pre-planned as a soap opera cliffhanger.

Dolas was practically a walking charm offensive. He was adored by everyone in the office, from the admin and HR teams to Venky and even the ops crew. His larger-than-life personality made him the go-to guy for laughs and good vibes. Whether it was sharing jokes with the admin girls or getting on Venky's good side, Dolas had a knack for making friends everywhere he went.

It was almost like he had some secret formula for staying in everyone's good books. Maybe he had a magic touch or just a really good sense of humor. Whatever it was, Dolas knew how to work it to his advantage, keeping him firmly in the office's inner circle. I couldn't help but marvel at how he managed to be so universally liked—he seemed to have cracked the code for office popularity.

That day, I was supposed to tag along with Dolas on his sales calls. We headed out for lunch with Poojary at Ratnagiri—no beer, no cinema, just business. Dolas was a sales pro. His clients respected him, and he had this killer line he'd use: "Maine jo ek baar commitment kar di, toh main apne aap ki bhi nahi sunta." ("Once I make a commitment, I don't even listen to myself.") It was his secret weapon for getting repeat orders.

But here's where Dolas really shined. At our last client meeting, he realized he was short of his target by over 2 lakhs. So, he sweet-talked the client into issuing a purchase order and a cheque for 2.5 lakhs. As we left, he leaned in and whispered, "This client's a gem. He gives me cheques for whatever amount I'm short of. They bounce later, but by then, I've hit my targets. The Ops team is too slow to catch on. By the time they do, I'm long gone."

I was impressed and a bit in awe. "Why would he do that?"

"Helps me meet my targets and keeps the Ops team busy. Win-win!" Dolas winked. Classic Dolas, always with a plan.

Back at the office, Dolas seemed to have a special spot in Venky's heart, sparking rumors of Marathi favoritism. But honestly, who could blame Venky? Dolas had a knack for winning people over.

One morning, while I was stressing over a loan application, Dolas walked in. I was a mess, and Dolas, in his infinite wisdom and relaxed demeanor, noticed. "What's wrong?" he asked, genuinely concerned.

"Just family stuff," I said, shrugging.

"Come on, spill," he insisted.

"I applied for a personal loan, but no luck. Need a guarantor."

Without missing a beat, Dolas said, "I'll be your guarantor. What's the amount?"

"4 lakhs," I replied hesitantly.

"No problem. Cheer up! Want some tea?" he asked, as if offering tea was the ultimate solution to my problems.

"But Dolas, you don't even know me that well."

"Planning to run away after getting the loan? I'll find you and kill you, you remember my name right" he laughed. "Now, let's have another cigarette. You're stressing me out."

And just like that, Dolas turned a tough day into one filled with humor and unexpected generosity.

"Kadu: The Office Gossip Machine"

Kadu sauntered into the office a bit later after I'd settled in. He was Poojary's old buddy from their previous gig, and Poojary vouched for him like he was the second coming. Venky took an immediate liking to Kadu.

Kadu, with his solid sales chops, picked up our product faster than a cheat day donut, needing zero training. He was the fourth musketeer in Poojary's team, and they clicked like childhood pals.

Kadu and Poojary had this uncanny knack for mimicking people, especially our boss Venky, behind his back. If you want the entire office to know something, tell Kadu and ask him to keep it a secret. It was like setting off a gossip grenade.

One morning, Kadu dropped a bombshell. Apparently, Luthra and his girlfriend Shalini were not just logging orders late at night; they were getting cozy in the washroom. The ops guy overheard some screams while he was trying to take a piss. I thought, "Lucky guy! Free live porn show." Honestly, if I were him, I'd probably be playing a solo symphony with my little brother Baburao too.

The ops guy also mentioned that Shalini wore a skirt and slit panties for easy access, he heard them talking about it. What the hell are slit panties? I had to Google that one.

Another gem from Kadu was about Dolas. He was bringing his girlfriend and her parents to the office to meet Venky. Not for blessings, but because it was an arranged marriage and they wanted proof that Dolas actually had a job at a reputed company like ours. I wanted to say, "Sweetheart, if you think sales are stable, let me introduce you to the concept of unemployment."

Kadu had this Zen-like calm. With both his parents being branch managers at a government bank, he knew he'd never need to hustle too hard. He spent his days chain-smoking like a chimney. I'm pretty sure he was the brains behind the chai sutta bar concept, which now is a billion dollar business in India.

Kadu had a secret talent that was more surprising than finding a unicorn in the office pantry: he could mimic a female voice perfectly. He used this gift to keep up a charade on GTalk, chatting up freshers who had recently joined the Jobs.Com team. His tactic? Chatting them up with a spare phone—because one phone just wasn't enough for his nocturnal escapades. Sometimes, these eager newbies would even top up his phone credit, eager for more of his "attention."

He'd invite them to meet him at Andheri West McDonald's, making them sweat it out in the heat, waiting for their "date" while he watched from a distance. After making them endure 25-30 minutes of their fast-food misery, he'd swoop in like a late-night delivery, asking with a straight face what they were doing hanging out by the Golden Arches.

"How do I know all this?" you ask. I am a curious soul, you see :) Well, we shared a computer, and guess what? His login credentials were as secure as a paper bag in a hurricane. The username was "Kadu" and the password was—drumroll, please—"password." Seriously, Kadu? With a password like that, even a toddler could break into your account.

Kadu, Dolas, and Poojary had regular drinking sessions, and after a while, they trusted me enough to invite me along. Over drinks, I asked Kadu why he didn't put in a bit more effort to rake in more incentives. He was a sales ninja, after all.

He laughed and said, "90% of people here are too busy working. They don't smoke, they don't drink, and on weekends they catch up on sleep. They might as well be dogs. Why be a human if you're not going to live it up?"

Wise words from a man who knew **how to enjoy life.**

"Srivastava: The Master of Excuses and Slip-ups"

Srivastav, Picture this: a guy from a humble family in UP, determined to rise in life by hook or by crook. He knew Kadu and Poojary from their previous gig, and was the last to join our motley crew. This dude rocked a tie, had his hair combed like a 1950s hero, and generously oiled it to the point where it dripped down his ears, giving his shirt an unintentional tie-dye look. He was obsessed with perfect sales attire, though. Most of us called him "Crow" because of his dark complexion. Not to sound like others, but I swear, he could've led a secret army of crows in Game of Thrones. He truly looked like he belonged to the crow family.

His voice was funny, like a cartoon character, and brushing his teeth seemed optional, resulting in a set of shiny yellow chompers. Magically, this guy had a girlfriend he was committed to, which baffled us daily. We struggled to impress girls with our 6-day work week and 9am to 9pm grind. How on earth did he manage it? Impossible!

Shrivastav usually rolled in late, claiming he had morning meetings. Kadu, our office gossip machine, knew Shrivastav's habits inside out. And remember, Kadu couldn't keep a secret if his life depended on it. So, naturally, the whole office knew Shrivastav had a girlfriend, which made everyone envious. But wait, there's more. Shrivastav wasn't just a master in romance; he was a pro at cracking interviews.

Back then, it was easier to lie about your experience or offer letters. All you needed was someone to vouch for you and a fake letter or salary slip. And Shrivastav was the Picasso of

this art. Kadu's fresh gossip was that before Shrivastav joined our team, he went for an interview for a Branch Manager position at another company. He faked his experience, claiming to be a Branch Manager at Monster.com, despite being a junior sales executive. Apparently, the interviewer was the ex-branch manager of Monster. When he asked Shrivastav, "I never saw you at Monster.com, and I was the regional manager," Shrivastav confidently shot back, "You need to start eating almonds; that might help your memory." Needless to say, he wasn't selected.

Shrivastav also had a unique talent for making excuses to skip work. His go-to excuse? Loose motions. And here's the irony: you can't call a person to the office if they claim to have loose motions—it's too risky for everyone around. Shrivastav knew this loophole too well. So whenever he wanted to bunk, he'd declare he had loose motions, leaving us no choice but to let him stay home. **This guy was a genius at dodging work and making it seem legit.**

"Chauhan and Sonali: A Love Story with a Side of Office Gossip and Creative Target Management"

Let me introduce you to Chauhan and Sonali, two stars in the office drama—though they were more like a soap opera and a circus rolled into one. Chauhan was the quintessential quiet guy, always in his own world, and never one to seek the limelight. He was so focused, I half expected him to start using a laser pointer to navigate his workday. On the flip side, Sonali was like a human confetti cannon—bright, bubbly, and impossible to ignore.

One day, Sonali managed to strike up a conversation with Kadu. Now, Kadu is the sort of person who treats secrets like he treats gossip—he's terrible at both. If you ask Kadu to keep a secret, you might as well shout it from the rooftops because the whole office will know within the hour. So, when Kadu got wind of Chauhan and Sonali's budding romance, you could bet your last stapler that it wasn't going to stay hush-hush for long.

Sure enough, the next day, everyone in the office was practically equipped with a new fact: Chauhan and Sonali were seeing each other. And just to make sure the rumor mill was in full swing, someone even managed to snap a photo of them kissing in an auto. I'm still baffled by who had the energy, time, and stealth skills to capture that perfect shot while both vehicles were in motion. Was there a secret paparazzi in the office? Did someone invest in a high-speed camera just for this?

So, as usual, the gossip train had left the station, and Chauhan came to me, looking like he'd just walked through a field of landmines. He asked me who might have spread the rumor. Now, I knew who the culprit was, but unlike Kadu, I had the magical ability to keep secrets. I pretended to be as clueless as a goldfish. Chauhan was all worked up about the potential fallout—apparently, if the girl's family caught wind of this affair, both Chauhan and Sonali were in for some serious trouble. Turns out Kadu's knack for disaster predictions was spot-on.

With the secret out, Chauhan and Sonali's covert office romance became public knowledge. Suddenly, they were free to exchange love-struck glances and gossip during office hours. The office was buzzing, but in a twisted way, it was kind of a blessing in disguise. They were still hitting their targets every month, and no one could fault their work ethic. It was like they were running a secret operation called "Operation: Keep Your Job and Your Relationship."

One day, Chauhan, who was now in full disclosure mode, opened up about their secret sauce for success. I asked him how they managed to achieve their targets without ever falling short. He leaned in like he was about to share the secret recipe for Coca-Cola and said, *"It's simple, really. We keep tabs on who's falling short, and we log the orders under their name. If we have extra orders, we save them for next month. That way, we hit our targets and avoid making Venky too happy with overachievement."*

I couldn't help but think, "Wow, that's ingenious!" It's like they'd cracked the code to office life: do just enough to survive without setting off the boss's radar. Balance is key, they said. They managed to stay out of the hot seat while keeping their romance alive. Brilliant, right? Not exactly my style, though. I was all about those incentives and cash bonuses.

So, Chauhan and Sonali: a pair who managed to juggle romance, targets, and office gossip with a flair that would make a circus performer proud. Their story is a reminder that sometimes, a bit of cleverness and a lot of gossip can make for the most interesting workdays.

The Boring Duo's Manish1 & Manish2 - HardWork Vs Smart Work

Manish1 and Manish2 were alike in a few ways—both wore formal clothes and spoke polished English. They were smart, no doubt, but one worked hard, while the other worked smart. Now, I'll be honest, talking about either of them is like watching paint dry, but for the sake of the lessons they taught me, here goes.

Let's start with Manish1—the hardworking guy. He lived in Mira Road, constantly running late for work, barely squeezing in 8-10 appointments a day. Yet, somehow, he made it work. His internal policy? Sell to every client, no matter what. He'd start pitching with numbers around 1.5 to 2 lakhs, and before the client even blinked, he'd drop it to 50k, just to make them buy something. And if that didn't work, he'd practically beg for a 10k deal. Honestly, sometimes it felt like clients gave him money just because they pitied him—a polished guy reduced to begging for scraps.

Every day, he was buried under paperwork, sitting with the ops guys, punching in orders. Despite all that, he hit 80-90% of his targets consistently. He'd been with the firm for two years, and my boss decided it was time to promote him. Why? Because he was the hardest working guy on the team. He even managed a small team—Srivastava (yes, the same guy we all pitied) and another equally useless soul whose name isn't even worth mentioning.

So, Manish1 had his own mountain of work, plus the burden of dragging these two along. Yet somehow, they barely managed to scrape together 4-5 lakhs of revenue. And they were always busy—like, ridiculously busy.

Now, onto Manish2—the smart worker. Nobody really knew where he lived because he barely spoke. This guy was so quiet, I'm sure he'd have no problem camouflaging for days like a sniper. You remember snipers and spotters, right? The ones who go days without eating or even blinking? That was Manish2 in the office.

He had just one team member, and they were rarely seen out of their cubicle. Busy with their laptops, they didn't bother with small talk. But Manish2 shared the top spot in the all-India sales ranking with Luthra, always switching between first and second place. He had around 20 clients, and that was it—those clients were his whole world.

Let me give you an example: he had HDFC Bank as a client, which meant every business connected to HDFC became his. HDFC Insurance, HDFC Securities, HDFC Mutual Fund—if it had "HDFC" on it, it was his.

After nagging him for days, I finally got to join him for two meetings. ***This guy was methodical. He didn't talk much—he just asked questions, gathered info, jotted notes, and that was it. The minute we got back to the office, he'd send a detailed email with the minutes of the meeting so he didn't miss a thing. He'd take 3-5 days to respond to client queries but never missed a deadline.***

He had this timesheet, supposedly from some sales guru, with four categories:

1. Urgent & Important
2. Urgent but Not Important
3. Important but Not Urgent
4. Not Urgent, Not Important.

He literally wrote everything into that sheet. If a friend pinged him on BBM, he'd log it in and decide when to respond. I always wondered—what if he needed to take a leak urgently? Yep, he'd probably log that too. And if his girlfriend wanted some action? Well, I'm still guessing on that one.

Manish2's average order value started at 4-5 lakhs, and he even held the record for the largest single order—12.5 lakhs. Impressive, right? He probably got bored with his own success. I tried being as boring as him once, but it didn't work. Maybe one day, I'll figure it out.

"Venky (The Boss): How to Manage People While Perfecting Your Flirting Skills"

Ah, Venky. If you ever wondered what a package deal of punctuality, tech obsession, and a dash of flirtation looks like, Venky is your guy. Standing at a modest 5'5" with a perpetually wicked smile, curly hair, and a French beard, he was the living proof that great things come in small, gadget-obsessed packages.

So, here's the deal with Venky: he was always on time. Like, if the office clock had a time machine, Venky would be there before it was even built. At 8:30 am sharp, he'd waltz in, usually with a new phone in hand. And let me tell you, Venky's love for gadgets was something to behold. He had this latest phone that could practically bend time and space, and then, for reasons known only to him, he kept an old Reliance phone. This phone was so indestructible that it could survive a nuclear apocalypse. Venky used it to show off his dramatic flair, throwing it around like it was a prop in a soap opera whenever he felt the need to express his frustration.

"Do you think I'm an idiot, you asshole?" he'd roar, chucking his unbreakable phone across the room. It was his way of saying, "I'm angry, but I'm too civilized to yell at you."

Venky was the epitome of a perfectionist. His Excel skills? Legendary. You'd think he invented VLOOKUP himself. His PowerPoint presentations were so slick, they could double as stand-up comedy routines. But when it came to managing people, Venky had a unique system:

1. **Level One:** He gave zero fucks to those who never hit their targets. No pressure at all. It's like they didn't even exist in his world.
2. **Level Two:** He lavished attention on those who met their targets. "Oh, good job!" he'd say, as if handing out gold stars in kindergarten.
3. **Level Three:** Now, this is where it got interesting. If you overachieved, you were a horse, not a pony. Venky would push you to achieve the whole team's shortfall, just to keep you on your toes. It was his way of saying, "Congratulations, now run a marathon."

Despite his tendency to make you feel like a circus performer, Venky was generous with incentives. Some of us were making triple our salaries in incentives alone. And speaking of perks, our team ranked No. 2 pan-India, which meant we got out-of-town trips. The top 10 teams got a lovely retreat to Alibaug, and if you were in the top 5, you got to go to Goa. Guess what? Everyone wanted Goa. It was like the Holy Grail of office trips.

But here's the kicker: Venky never actually sold anything. Yep, he had us doing the heavy lifting while he reaped the rewards. Whenever I asked him to join me for a sales meeting, he had a million excuses. "Oh, I've got a meeting," or "I'm tied up with some admin stuff." Little did I know, this would turn out to be a lesson in itself—how to manage a team without being the star performer.

Now, let's not forget Venky's other talent: flirtation. His interactions with the office's female staff were the stuff of legends. Rumor had it that he was involved in a fling with one of the admin girls. And who was spreading these spicy tidbits? None other than Kadu, of course.

At the end of every month, after closing time, Venky would treat the top performers to a beer—or two if you were his favorite. Dolas and Luthra, for instance, were practically guaranteed extra beers. Venky went so far as to warmly welcome Dolas's future in-laws, treating them like royalty. He even ordered tea and snacks for them and cracked jokes like he was Dolas's big brother rather than his boss.

Our team's success earned us a trip to a five-star property in Alibaug. And while we were all excited about the getaway, Venky was busy flirting with the admin girl. It was like watching a soap opera unfold in real-time.

*So, there you have it. Venky: the man who could **manage people, gadgets, and flirtation with equal flair, all while avoiding the actual selling.***

Alibaug Trip: The Jimmy's Beach Resort

Morning everyone arrived around 8 am at the office, and miraculously, no one was late. Venky had made it clear: the bus leaves at 8:30 am sharp. People knew better than to test his patience.

As the backbenchers, Poojary, Kadu, and Dolas snagged the last two seats. This also helped hide the alcohol we mixed with water. We were pros at this, sipping whiskey in bars until we ran out and then continuing the party with our secret stash. Master planner Poojary had already orchestrated our covert operation for the trip, ensuring our "hydration" until we reached our destination.

The bus started on time, and we began our usual antics for the long 3-4 hour journey. The girl gang up front kicked off an antakshari session, while we entertained ourselves with Kadu's brilliant idea: Rajinikanth one-liner jokes.

"When Rajinikanth calls 100, it's to ask if everything is okay!" Kadu began.

"Rajinikanth knows Victoria's Secret!" Dolas chimed in.

"Harvard got its MBA from Rajinikanth!" Jain added.

"Rajinikanth can delete the Recycle Bin!" I hesitantly threw in.

The final, winning joke came from Poojary: "Anaconda movie was shot inside Rajinikanth's underwear." Poojary was declared the undisputed winner, and we all clapped.

We arrived at Jimmy's Beach Resort, a luxurious 5-star property nestled in a coconut grove on the pristine Varsoli beach. This place was a perfect getaway, far from the hustle and bustle of everyday life. With private villas, a private beach, and an exclusive swimming area, it was the ideal spot for a holiday or business meeting. Our elegant and contemporary rooms welcomed us with a warm and cozy ambiance. Each room offered spectacular views of either the sea, pool, or garden, assuring us a truly laid-back holiday experience.

We arrived at Jimmy's and were greeted warmly by their team. After sipping our welcome drinks and munching on cookies, we were assigned rooms. I had no choice but to room with Jain, which turned out to be more enlightening than expected.

After changing, I headed to Poojary and Dolas' room next door. Dolas opened the door, wearing a body-hugging t-shirt and shorts.

"I am a bird, I like to fly, la la la la…" Poojary was singing in the bathroom.

"Is Poojary taking a bath?"

"Nope, he's flying in the bathtub. It's been 40 minutes," Dolas replied, rolling his eyes.

"Hey Dubey, the door is open. Come inside," Poojary called out.

I hesitantly opened the door to find him wrapped in bubbles like a princess. He even had bubbles on his head; all he needed was a rainbow unicorn to complete the scene.

Dolas, meanwhile, was on a video call with his fiancée for what seemed like the third time that day, chirping like a teenage lovebird. "Aww, honey, I miss you too!" He could talk to her for 40 minutes straight without missing a beat, each time with the same teenage enthusiasm.

After another 20 minutes of changing clothes, we headed for lunch. The evening party was scheduled to start at 8 pm, with a dress code of black. The place was drenched in alcohol.

Poojary approached me with a glass of beer, and we both said, "Alcohola!"

"Isn't that Jain drinking whiskey? I thought he doesn't drink," I remarked.

"He doesn't drink with his own money," Kadu joined us.

Dolas strutted over in a shiny black shirt with three buttons open, holding a pint of beer.

We all started dancing to the "Kaminey" song, and it felt like we all understood that this song was more of a statement than just a dance number. Dolas asked the DJ to play a few Salman Khan tracks so he could show off his moves. Poojary and Kadu got even more excited when the DJ played songs from "Satya."

English tracks started playing, and Luthra and Shalini were engaged in a dance that was borderline scandalous—they definitely had chemistry on the floor. Chauhan and Sonal were so in sync, you'd think they were rehearsing for a wedding dance routine.

Meanwhile, the girls were busting out their moves to every hit from "Baby Doll" to "Chikni Chameli" and "Fevicol." It was like watching a professional dance-off, and we were just there with our jaws on the floor, feeling like we'd stumbled into a Dance India Dance audition.

"Kajra Re" and "Aa Ante Amalapuram" made everyone equal on the dance floor. To my surprise, I saw Venky matching steps with the HR girl. It seemed like everyone was giving their best performance.

Jain, on the other hand, was a walking alcohol advertisement. He'd clearly had a few too many and decided to play the role of the office perv, tailing a young recruit around like a bad sequel to a stalker film. His intentions were so obvious, even the office plants were giving him side-eye. Luckily, Dolas swooped in and put an end to the sleazy antics, or else I might've had to channel my inner superhero and give Jain a punch that would've made his liver rethink its life choices.

Jain drank more than half a bottle and started dancing like he was at a rave. By the end, he was crowned the last man standing, earning claps and cheers.

"Anyone up for a smoke?" Asked Poojary - Kadu, Dolas, Poojary, and I moved out, followed by Jain.

Poojary pulled out a cigar. "Anyone want a puff? It's Cuban." He conveniently omitted the fact that it had hashish mixed in. Driven by excitement, I took the first puff, passing it to Jain, who eagerly took three.

"Go slow, bro!" Dolas whispered.

"It's okay, let him enjoy it. More fun for us," Poojary grinned.

"Venky will kill us if we don't wake up on time tomorrow," I reminded everyone.

Jain opened his pants, pulled out his "Baburao," and said, "Venky, get up! You've been sleeping all day."

"Did he just call Venky a dick?" I asked, dumbfounded.

"Yes, and he waved it around saying, 'Venky, say hello to everyone. Let's go find Luthra and ask him to join us,'" Jain suggested.

Kadu didn't try the cigar but vowed to be part of our sins and crimes, promising to keep it a secret.

"Shall we sneak in like ghosts and scare Luthra through the window?" I proposed.

"Great idea! I'll get some bedsheets," Poojary said, quickly returning with four white sheets.

We stealthily approached Luthra's ground floor room. Dolas promised he could open the window.

We reached behind Luthra's room, and surprise—the window was already open.

"He must be smoking and forgot to close it. That's our luck," Poojary whispered.

"Dolas, you go first," I suggested.

Dolas climbed in, and I followed. We pulled back the curtain and jumped inside, only to find Shalini naked, jumping off the bed. In the three seconds before she covered herself, we noticed everything—her perfectly rounded tits and ass curves that would make a Kardashian jealous.

"What the fuck are you guys doing here?" Luthra shouted.

"Oh, I'm sorry," I said, jumping right back out.

"How were we supposed to know he was having a midnight rodeo with his cowgirl?" I muttered. "Where's his partner? Let me guess—Chauhan?" Ohh so Shalini was Sonali's room partner, I guess.

Dolas emerged next, sporting a satisfied smirk.

"Who was riding Luthra's horse? A cowgirl... hehehe," Kadu chuckled, already compiling a fresh batch of gossip for the morning.

"Nobody tells anyone what happened here," Poojary commanded. "We are brothers, sworn by oath."

"What oath?" Jain asked.

"It's a tribal thing. I'll teach you all. Find four big sticks."

After gathering the sticks, Poojary produced a bottle of cooking oil from his room.

"Where the hell did that come from?" Kadu asked.

"Plan, bro! Plan," Poojary responded.

We crossed the small gate connecting the resort to a private beach, walking a bit with our mobile flashlights.

"We'll dance around the fire and be sworn brothers, keeping our secrets forever," Poojary declared.

We wrapped the sheets around the sticks, soaked them in oil, and lit them on fire. The four sticks were placed in the middle, and we danced around them in silence, our faces contorted in mock anger.

Jain, clearly inspired, said, "We are brothers, we all sleep together!" and tossed our room keys into the ocean.

High on alcohol, emotions, and hashish, we danced until the cigar was done, then headed back to our rooms.

Poojary and Kadu shared a bed, Dolas slept beside Jain, and I took the corner. Around midnight, I woke up to a strange noise.

"Tul tul tul tul... tul tul tul tul..." Jain was peeing on Dolas' face.

"What the fuck are you doing?" I shouted.

"Can't you see? I'm peeing. Join me if you want."

After he was done, Jain bounced back on the bed. I moved to join Poojary and Kadu, who had seen everything but said nothing, giving me space to sleep.

The next morning, I freshened up and joined the breakfast table. Luthra ignored my greeting, while Venky gave me a knowing smile. Kadu had a poker face, betraying nothing. So much for brotherhood—the dance was for nothing. "This fucker told everything," I murmured.

"Morning, everyone!" Jain greeted cheerfully.

"Morning, Jain. I heard you guys had a hell of a night, especially you," Venky replied, hinting that Kadu had spilled the beans about "Baburao."

Jain started filling his plate with food as if he planned to eat everything.

Dolas joined the table, his face a billboard for "HANGOVER." He licked his fingers and wiped his face with his hands, saying, "I think I took a dip in the ocean last night." I guess he meant his face had salt on it.

Kadu shouted, "Jungle mein nacha mor, kisne dekha?" ("Who saw the peacock dancing in the forest?") Everyone replied, "Dubey ne!" We burst into laughter, with several of us collapsing on the floor, rolling with laughter.

Dolas was clueless, while Kadu maintained his poker face. "I am sworn to keep secrets, brother. I didn't do it," he seemed to say.

Jain knew he was fucked—Dolas was about to unleash every muscle in his body. He abandoned his plate mid-bite and ran like hell!

We took the bus back home in the evening, already planning our next trip to Goa. To get there, we needed to hit our targets. **Time to buckle down and start selling!**

Month end, judgment day, let's qualify for GOA.

We had 15 days left to conquer our sales targets after the Alibaug trip. We'd racked up 44 Lakhs out of our 80 Lakhs target. Luthra had hit his numbers, but I was floundering. With a 6 lac target, my straightforward, hard-working approach seemed to be losing to those sneaky shortcuts.

A week before, Dolas had gotten engaged to Trupti and was parading his ring like he'd just won the lottery. He spent 30-40 minutes on video calls during office hours, introducing Trupti to everyone—yes, even the office plants. Poojary warned him, "This could come back to haunt you!" How prophetic.

Most folks showed up on time today. Venky wore his usual "I've been chewing on a lemon" face, affectionately dubbed the "Baburao" look by Jain. The smoking gang was busy on the stairs, working on their life expectancy. I joined them, thinking if they're heading to hell, I might as well have some fun on the way. Ignoring the grim photo of a dying man on the wall—much like how we ignore our own farts but always catch others'—I wondered why we cared so much about one and not the other.

Poojary was in his element, dissecting the symphonies of farts. Mine, he claimed, sounded like a bullet—a fat, hurried bullet—because I was always trying to hide something. He then mused about how Srivastav might kill his girlfriend with his "fuski's" and why Venky was perpetually angry. "He's not getting his farts," Poojary quipped, "so constipation is making him furious."

Enter Kadu with the juiciest scoop of the day: Luthra had apparently ordered a BDSM kit, gearing up for what he imagined would be a wild adventure with Shalini on their Goa trip. Now, just picture this—Luthra, the "master negotiator," clumsily trying to figure out ropes and cuffs like he's assembling IKEA furniture, while poor Shalini, blindfolded and handcuffed, is wondering if she's signed up for a yoga class gone horribly wrong. Meanwhile, Dubey is off in his own world, dreaming of perfecting the moves on Shalini himself, staring through a peephole like a budget 007, all while Dolas and Dubey can barely contain their snickering at the impending disaster. Comedy gold was about to unfold!

A peon interrupted our gossip session to let us know Venky was on the warpath, looking for Poojary. We all scrambled back to our desks, ready for battle. Venky, in his classic foul mood, stormed over to Abhishek, demanding to know where Srivastav was. Kadu, playing innocent, shrugged. "No idea." Venky stormed off to the ops team to check our shortfall.

Dolas was seated at his desk, looking as if he'd just been smacked with a steel rod. I asked Poojary about Dolas, and he said, "His girlfriend fought with him over a girl who was too cozy with Dolas during Trupti's introduction. Trupti's now meeting her male friends. Dolas really screwed himself over—his dick must be too long!" Poojary's disdain was palpable.

Chauhan and Sonali, having hit 90% of their targets, waved goodbye with smiles as they left. Kadu and I, facing our shortfall, decided to skip the Ratnagiri lunch and head straight to appointments today.

Shalini, seated proudly at her desk, had overachieved her targets. Like Luthra, she was a top performer, and their bold personalities clearly made sparks fly.

Luthra had already left, and Dolas and Poojary headed out together. Kadu, still savoring his coffee, needed a nudge from me about the time—11 am, and Venky's mood was about to explode.

We took an auto rickshaw to Andheri. On the way, I asked Kadu about Srivastav. "Loose motions," Kadu replied. "He's convinced Venky will buy that excuse at month's end, even while he's busy with his girlfriend in a lodge. He's toast."

"Is he worried about losing his job?" I asked.

"He says he'll find another one," Kadu answered.

Arriving in Andheri, we split for our appointments. At 3 pm, Poojary called, saying he was at McDonald's, waiting for a friend who wasn't showing up. I joined him, and Kadu made a surprise visit 10-15 minutes later, asking what we were doing there. I played along, saying Poojary's friend had bailed.

Poojary bragged, "She's not a friend, just a weekend fling."

"Devil knows best," I thought, watching Kadu sympathize with Poojary's sweaty predicament.

"What's the plan?" I asked.

"I don't know," Poojary admitted, "I'm nowhere near my targets, and the team targets are a joke."

"Poojary is my supervisor," I reminded him.

Kadu suggested, "How about a beer?"

"No way," I said,

"Venky's going to screw us anyway. Better to drink up before that happens!" Poojary countered.

"Never say no to beer!" -Kadu suggested again.

We ended up at Ratnagiri, drinking beer with no hope of hitting GOA. Afterward, we went to Sona Cinema for the 4.00 pm show. figuring we'd be out by 6:30pm and could report to the office by 7:00 pm. We turned off our phones to avoid interruptions, except for Poojary, who hoped Dolas might call and join us.

At 5:30 pm, Venky called Poojary. His face turned ghostly pale, and he scurried outside. Venky asked, "How's the movie?"

Poojary, sounding like a deer caught in headlights, stammered, "Movie? What movie? I'm not watching any movie!"

Venky, with the firmness of a drill sergeant, replied, "So, what are Dubey and Kadu doing with you in the theater?" A wild guess, but right on the money since our phones were off and he smelled our nonsense from a mile away.

Poojary, sweating bullets, blurted out, "I'm sorry, Venky. I was under pressure! They forced me to join the movie!"

Yeah, right. Forced him to watch a movie—next thing you know, he'll claim he was kidnapped by aliens too.

Our fates were sealed. We trudged back to the office, dreading the inevitable.

I imagined Luthra handing his BDSM kit to Venky for real-life torture. Venky would relish every moment, whipping our bums while we were tied up and bending over his desk. Jain and others would have a field day laughing at our misery.

Returning to the office, Venky summoned us one by one. He grilled me for 20 minutes, demanding I leave and come back with an order.

I knew Venky was on the edge, ready to unleash his trademark nagging, and today was the perfect storm for it. He has this amusing habit: the cheap phone on the left, the expensive one on the right—his little perfectionist ritual. When his frustration hit its peak, he hurled the phone onto the floor with a dramatic *thud* that could have registered on the Richter scale.

Of course, it was his brand-new LG that took the fall. The moment it hit the ground, his face went white as a ghost, and he screamed, "Ahhh, my phone!"—as if it were a rare artifact rather than just another gadget. The old, battered phones never got such a fuss when he tossed them.

Meanwhile, I was facing a 1.5 Lakhs shortfall, and adding "piss off Venky even more" to my plate was not an option. With looming bills and family responsibilities, I made my hasty exit, hoping to avoid making things worse.

On the way back, I met Dolas, whose chirpiness had vanished. With girlfriend issues and unmet targets, he was a mess.

I waited an hour in a restaurant, then returned to the office. The atmosphere was tense when I arrived. Poojary and Kadu had nothing. Dolas came in with a 2 lac purchase order, but he wasn't celebrating.

He gave the order form to the ops team, and Venky was informed. Venky was still 12 Lakhs short of our 80 Lakhs target, and he took the opportunity to deliver his golden speech. He ranted about having an "army of eunuchs," "good for nothing," and how he relied on us idiots.

"These three clowns are watching a movie while one's screwing his girlfriend in a lodge," he fumed.

I asked Venky for two minutes in his cabin.

"12.8 Lakhs short—got a magic wand?" Venky growled.

"No magic wand," I said, "but I do have a PO." I pulled out a 16 lac order form and slapped it on his desk.

Venky's eyes widened. "Better have an advance check for this," he said.

I handed him a signed and stamped cheque.

"You had this the whole time and were just enjoying our frustrations?" he asked.

"I closed the deal five days ago, but the check came in today," I said with a wicked smile.

Venky's face lit up. "We're going to GOA!" He burst out of his cabin, shouting, "We're going to GOA! Dubey worked his magic. Promotion time for Dubey!"

"You switched my phone's right?" Venky asked, his voice dripping with faux sweetness. I looked him dead in the eye and denied it, because obviously, it's my life's mission to mess with his meticulously organized gadgets.

Manish2 smiled quietly, never one to celebrate. It felt like a challenge was coming my way. Or maybe I caught onto something he never thought I'd pick up so fast!

We celebrated like we'd been resurrected from a graveyard to a rave party. I was invited to a beer session with Venky and a select few—part of the elite club. I felt proud.

After 30 minutes, I joined Poojary and others at a bar, where we drank until 2 am. Dolas left early, still upset.

I took an auto back to Mira Road, **proudly shouting, "GOA!"**

Venky had booked our flights for the next evening. At the airport, we were early, but Srivastav and Dolas were missing. Venky was restless. "It's okay if Srivastav doesn't show, but Dolas—his phone's off!" Venky said.

Poojary tried to reach Dolas. "Yesterday, he called me 3-4 times, upset about his girl not coming home. I spoke to him for a bit, then put my phone on silent and went to sleep. This morning, I saw 20+ missed calls. Now his phone's off."

Poojary's phone rang. It was Dolas.

Dolas: "Where are you? Oh, sorry, yes Aunty. What? When?"

The call ended, and Poojary's face drained of color. He could barely manage to speak. "Dolas' mother called. Dolas hanged himself last night."

Silence after Dolas...

We had to cancel our plans for Goa. Instead, we found ourselves returning to attend Dolas' funeral. The fun we once shared seemed to vanish the moment he left us. It didn't feel the same anymore, not without him.

Soon, I found myself dreading going to the office each day. Walking in felt like a painful reminder of what had happened. The atmosphere was heavy with his absence, and we all missed him—more than we could have imagined. We had grown close, much closer than I ever realized. His absence left a void that made it harder to keep going, as if the heart of our little world had been taken away.

The next chapter: Time to execute what I learned...

A few months later, I moved on. After leaving Jobs.com, I joined Business.com as a Sales Manager, leading a small team of 4-5 people. This was my first real experience managing a team, and funny enough, **it was the skills I picked up from Srivastava, of all people, that helped me crack the interview.** He was a master at clearing them, even if it meant faking his papers—experience letters, salary slips, the works. I leaned on him for help and ended up with a salary hike of over 100%.

I guess I'm no saint either, after all.

"Bhutta: The Quick-Learner Who Turned Copy-Paste into a Sales Superpower"

Butta was a fresh MBA grad from my alma mater, a bright-eyed kid who walked into our office for an interview, full of passion and determination. He was eager to join our "prestigious" organization—a place where tradition meets, well, the kind of old-school charm that only a newspaper company can offer. Our newspaper might sell fewer copies than a roadside tea stall has customers, but in the market, it was considered the gold standard for content and authenticity. Credibility, right?

I played the role of the seasoned interviewer, offering him a cup of tea before diving into the basics. "What are the 4Ps of marketing?" "How is sales different from marketing?"—the usual MBA fare. But then, channeling my inner Venky, I threw him a curveball: "If you could have any superhero power, what would it be?"

Butta thought for a moment and said, "I'd want to fly. Partly because I hate traffic, and also because I've never seen things from a bird's-eye view before—except from an airplane window. Plus, it'd be cool to travel to new places quickly."

In my head, I chuckled. "Kid, if you're getting into sales, the only flying you'll do is from one client meeting to the next. But hey, if you like traveling, you might just survive in this job."

Next, I hit him with the classic sales test: "Sell me this pen." He looked me straight in the eye and asked, "Why do you need one?" I said, "To write something." He didn't miss a beat: "Great, how much are you willing to pay?" And just like that, I knew this kid had what it took.

Butta, ever the negotiator, tried to squeeze out a better salary before we wrapped up. I dangled the usual carrot: "You'll get more incentives and a promotion before the year's out if you prove yourself." With that, we sealed the deal. He was hired.

He showed up a couple of days later, bright and early at 9:30 AM. Little did he know, I'm an 8:30 AM guy—already on my second cup of coffee and halfway through planning my day by then. I welcomed him with a coffee, and he was surprised to see me there so early. After all, who expects the boss to be the first one in?

Butta's face dropped when he saw the office—think Raju's home from *3 Idiots*, but with more dust. Piles of newspapers were strewn across every desk. The computers were ancient, the kind that make you nostalgic for the early 2000s. The staff, some of whom had been there for 20+ years, typed at a pace that would make a snail seem fast, using their index fingers. Many of them wore such thick glasses that if they stepped into the sunlight, they'd risk setting their eyebrows on fire from the magnifying effect.

The office was caked in rust and dust, so much so that touching anything practically guaranteed you'd need a tetanus shot. If we ever decided to clean up, the money vendors would demand for the job would probably bankrupt us.

I showed him to his desk, which was strategically located in the middle of what could only be described as a relic from another era. A small corner with a laptop that was old and slow enough to be considered vintage. I had already put in a request with IT to upgrade the RAM, but let's be real, that might happen in the next financial year if we're lucky. If he'd had the option, Butta would've brought his own laptop, but our company had a strict policy on using only "secured" company-issued devices. You'd think we were guarding top-secret government data at Business.Com.

The first thing I asked was, "Do you smoke?" He quickly responded, "No, Sir, I don't." Still, I took him down to the tea stall for an unofficial sutta talk, where all the real business happens.

By lunchtime, Butta had already read the newspaper three times over and was probably questioning every life choice that had led him to this point. I decided to lift his spirits. "Butta, let's go grab some lunch. My treat." His face lit up like a kid who'd just been told he could have dessert before dinner. Standing at 5'8" and tipping the scales at around 90 kg, it was clear that food was his go-to comfort zone.

I took him to a local Chinese restaurant, Royal Lunch Home, that was a favorite of mine. The food was fantastic—authentic Chinese with some Indian twists. Butta loved it. The place also served beer, but I refrained from offering any. It was his first day, after all; there would be plenty of time for that later.

Butta was a quick learner. He had this incredible talent for copy-pasting—not just in documents, but in real life. He could mimic anyone's speech patterns and mannerisms with scary accuracy. He picked up my sales pitch in record time, and it was mandatory to perfect it in our team. Unless I was convinced of their tone, voice modulation, and ability to make it sound natural, no one was allowed to call clients. I'm a stickler for that.

It was also mandatory to wear ties when meeting clients—especially corporate ones. However, when meeting with media agencies, we had to go mostly casual. They felt we were aliens if we showed up in formal attire. So, most days, we carried extra clothes if we had back-to-back meetings with corporations and media agencies. Saturdays were an exception; the team could wear formal Polo T-shirts to the office.

Within a week, Butta had perfected his sales pitch, learned how to whip up a 20-slide PPT in under 10 minutes, and mastered our 30-minute turnaround time for client proposals. We had set strict turnaround times (TATs) to revert back on any proposal request, unless it was a custom requirement for a larger client. In those cases, I would attend to it personally, sparing our boss, who was infamous for taking at least 10 days to respond to anything.

Butta was constantly impressed by my rapport-building skills with clients and would pepper me with questions about how I became their buddy so quickly. I had a few tricks up my sleeve. One of the most effective? Drinking sessions after work. There's something about sharing a drink that breaks down barriers and turns clients into friends. I also had a habit of carrying a few cigarettes, even though I wasn't a regular smoker. I'd invite busy clients for a quick smoke, and trust me, no one ever said no to a free cigarette. We'd get our follow-ups done, and sometimes even seal deals while we puffed away.

Butta was quick to catch on. He didn't smoke, but soon enough, he started carrying a packet of cigarettes for clients. When I asked about it, he grinned and said, "I don't smoke, Boss, but there's no harm in giving them company." To my surprise, he carried three different brands of cigarettes in one packet. Talk about being prepared!

Butta also shared my love for gaming, so I helped him set up a headset that supported the best gaming experience. Of course, I'd already cracked a few hacks to play games on our office laptops and upgraded the RAM to support the graphics. Soon, our side of the cabin looked like a tech-savvy hangout spot—lightyears ahead of the rest of the old-school office. We laughed, joked, played games, dialed clients, fixed appointments, and cracked deals. The ghostly silence of the place turned into a lively buzz. It was like having a small pub inside a library—the only thing missing was the doors.

Before long, Butta became my right-hand man. He followed my lead on everything, from creating error-free PPTs and Excel sheets to mastering VLOOKUP—skills I'd honed under Venky's watchful eye. I was so particular about details that I could tell the font size and family used in a PPT slide just by glancing at it. If it differed on the next slide, I'd catch it and make the necessary corrections. They started calling me Aamir Khan for my perfectionist tendencies.

Butta was a fast learner with a knack for copying in real life, and I knew that would take him far. He was going places—I was sure of it.

Siddu From Tiffins to Targets

Siddu, who came to us through Kadu's recommendation, was in desperate need of a job. Kadu asked me to lend a hand, and I couldn't say no. Siddu had the essential traits every good salesperson should have—hard work, dedication, discipline, and focus. The rest, like how not to spill coffee during a pitch, could be taught. One of his best skills? Doing exactly what he's told. He trusted my business instincts like a soldier trusts his general.

Hailing from Thane City, a quintessential Marathi hub, Siddu was a South Indian who spoke Marathi fluently. A die-hard fan of healthy living, he was religiously committed to a strict diet. His tiffin? An apple, a few nuts, and the secret ingredient—discipline, all packed in a small box. He ate every two hours and often quoted Rujuta Diwekar, the celebrity dietician, saying, "Rujuta aunty told me to stay disciplined." And yes, he read her book for an hour daily, every single day, as if it were the Bhagavad Gita.

Now, you've heard that women gossip, right? Well, they've got nothing on Siddu. He could out-gossip any Kaku Bai in our sales team. Lunch was his prime time for exchanging juicy tidbits, which, I suspect, helped him digest his food better. Kadu, the master of spreading news, had clearly rubbed off on Siddu. The only difference? Siddu stayed away from drinking and smoking.

Two months into his job at Business.Com, Siddu was supposed to hit a monthly target of 2 lakh as per my boss's orders. But I upped it to 3 lakhs, because why not? I had a knack for predicting revenue and could tell who would perform just by looking at their past numbers, current meetings, and future projections. Sadly, Siddu was more of a sitting duck. I even closed a few deals myself and credited them to his name, just to keep my boss off his back.

My Boss - Gotya: The Blame Game Master

Enter Gautam—aka Gotya—the blamer, the survivor, the chameleon who could change colors faster than you could say, "I'm fired." Gotya was a rare breed, capable of shifting his emotions in seconds. I remember once, Singh, my Delhi counterpart, was getting a verbal thrashing from Gotya—full of MCs and BCs—when suddenly, Gotya's phone rang. It was our CEO. With a switch as smooth as butter, he answered, "Yes Sir, no problem Sir, I'm here for you." The moment he hung up, he was back to abusing Singh. It was like watching a chameleon change color in real-time.

Thanks to Gotya's charming personality, two team members had already secured new jobs, while a third was on the verge of being fired. I'd only been in the system for four months, and already, things were falling apart faster than a cheap deck of cards. My six-person team was down to three, and targets were rising like the summer heat.

Siddu was assigned to handle PSU and NBFS clients, mainly spending his time at banks like SBI, Bank of India, Union Bank, and LIC. His daily routine? Sit at each of these offices, meet the PR teams, and try to close deals—without questioning a thing.

The CEO Showdown

One day, as I sat at my desk, I got a call from the CEO's office. I was summoned, and my heart raced faster than Gotya could shift blame. I walked into the CEO's cabin to find Gotya already there. The CEO asked, "Dubey, do you know why you're here?" Clueless, I replied, "No Sir."

With more authority, he said, "Gautam informed me that 2-3 people have left the team since you joined. Seems like managing a team is new to you, or maybe you're just not cut out for it. Your target is 35 lakhs this quarter."

Gotya, always eager to point fingers, nodded in agreement. The CEO asked, "What's your plan?" My mind was racing, but I had nothing concrete. I finally said, "Sir, since this is our first conversation in four months, I have no idea what image you have of me. But give me 90 days to prove my worth. After all, even a PIP takes 30 days & 60 days of official notice before you can fire someone."

The CEO nodded, and Gotya kept quiet. "What's your plan?" the CEO asked again. I responded, "Honestly, I don't have one yet. It may take 2-3 days to formulate. But in the meantime, I need three things from you. First, weekly reports shared with both you and Mr. Gautam, with a 10-minute discussion with you if possible. Second, a quicker turnaround on proposals—3 days instead of the usual 7-10. Third, if I hit the 35 lakh target with the same team, we should get a trip out of Mumbai, sponsored by the company, 10% flat incentive and a 30% raise during the annual appraisal. Plus, two more hires of my choice."

The CEO, a seasoned player, asked, "And if you don't?" I replied, "Then you can fire me without any notice—my ass belongs to you." Gotya tried to downplay the raise and incentive, but the CEO, smelling something rotten, firmed up the terms to 7.5% incentive and 20% appraisal raise. And you can plan a trip for GOA, if that's okay!

As I left the meeting, Gotya was furious, clearly hoping I'd be canned so he could pin everything on me. Bhutta and Siddu were waiting outside, having somehow caught wind of the showdown. Bhutta asked softly, "All okay, Boss?" I replied, "Gotya's an asshole, but we have to hit our targets no matter what."

Siddu, clueless as always but ever obedient, said, "We'll get it done. Just tell me what to do." With no clear plan in mind, I said, "Tonight, we're watching a movie—'300: The Spartans Story.'" If we were going to fight, we might as well get some inspiration from the best.

Let's Prepare for Battle

We had a battle ahead but no plan. So, the first step was obvious—make one! Simple, right? But for any battle plan to work, my soldiers (read: team) needed to be on the same page. Same mindset, same goal. So, what did we do? We decided to bond over drinks and a movie night. Genius, I know.

I sneaked a "water" bottle into the theater. Spoiler alert: it wasn't water, it was vodka. Trust me, it works. Try it sometime! We ordered three Sprite glasses, mixed in the vodka, and watched Gerard Butler lead his team into a suicide mission. As I watched, I felt like my situation was pretty similar. Only, instead of my life, it was my job on the line. A family to feed, a brother & sister to educate and a son to raise. Yep, no pressure. I whispered to myself the famous quote from Muhammad Ali: "We can't be brave without fear."

By the time the movie ended, we were riding high on emotions…and alcohol. Bhutta, with his classic grin, asked, "What's the plan, Boss?" I reminded him, "No business talk over drinks!" Siddu nodded in agreement.

That night, sleep wasn't my friend. I spent the next morning jotting down my thoughts on sticky notes. After a few coffees and a self-critique session (because I'm my biggest critic, FYI), I had a plan. One shot to get it right, so I better hit the bullseye.

The Next Morning

"Take a seat, guys," I told Bhutta and Siddu. "I have a target for this quarter, and there are rewards tied to it."

"Let's start with the rewards!" Bhutta, the eager one, jumped in.

"Alright, if we hit the target, we're going to GOA. Fully sponsored."

Both in unison: "GOA? Really?"

Memories of me screaming "GOA" from an auto when I hit my targets flashed by.

"Yes, and you'll also get a 7.5% net incentive plus a 20% annual raise next April."

Both: "Wait, WHAT? How did you pull that off?"

"I just accepted the target," I smirked.

"Okay, but how much is the target?" Siddu asked, as Bhutta leaned in curiously.

"35 lakhs for the quarter."

Their excitement faded. "That's huge, boss. What if we don't make it?" Siddu asked.
"I'll lose my job," I said, matter-of-factly. "And I can't guarantee you'll keep yours either."

"That's a massive gamble. What's the plan?" Bhutta asked.

I pulled out my sticky notes and laid it all out.

"Projecting Success: The Sales Plan"

Step 1: We target specific accounts—big ones. No more wasting time on small fries. We're going after clients with deep pockets, starting with banks, PSUs, mutual funds, insurance companies, and our loyal newspaper clients. Low-hanging fruit to get us rolling.

Both nodded in agreement.

Step 2: We're building direct relationships with clients, not just relying on agencies. If the client is Raymond's, we're meeting with their head of marketing. Agencies will be looped in, but they won't be our only touchpoint. And after every meeting, we'll send detailed minutes with clear action steps. And yes, CC me on all of it.

Siddu chimed in, "Can I ask a question now or wait till the end?"

"One more step, and then we'll talk."

Step 3: We're using a projection and time management sheet, which we'll follow religiously. I might even do surprise checks, so be warned. I'll personally handle the big-ticket proposals—none of them are going to Gautam. I'll send him some useless client requests just to keep him busy.

"Alright, Siddu. Go ahead."

"Here's the problem," Siddu started. "Gautam's your boss, which makes him my 'super boss,' and he interferes in everything. He constantly asks about clients, and when I tell him, he makes me call them ten times until they stop answering. It's happening with most of my clients."

"Same here, boss," Bhutta added. "That's why I stopped telling him which clients are positive. Sometimes, I don't even mention their names."

I grinned. "Brilliant! Let's make that part of our unofficial strategy—keep Gautam in the dark. He's a survivor; he'll need someone to blame when things go south."

I opened my projection sheet. "See this? We'll have hot, warm, and cold clients with amounts and closure dates against them.

For clarity between us:

- A **Hot Client** is one who has given verbal confirmation after negotiations and is clear on the amount they will invest in Business.Com.
- A **Warm Client** is one who has accepted the proposal, completed negotiations, but has not yet confirmed payment.
- A **Cold Client** is someone who has requested a proposal but hasn't responded or is avoiding our calls and emails.

We'll have two versions of projection sheets: Sheet 1 for Gautam and Sheet 3 for us. **In ours, everything will be accurate. In his, we'll flip the script. Cold clients become hot, hot clients turn cold. Have fun with it."**

Siddu looked confused at first, but Bhutta caught on immediately. After just one more explanation, Siddu was right on track!

Siddu hesitated, "But boss… lying isn't ethical, right?"

I smiled. "Neither is getting fired. Your call."

"So anytime Gautam asks about clients, give him the cold ones that won't convert. Be vague about the ones that will. He'll never bother with the cold leads anyway."

"Alright, what do you guys say?" I asked.

"We're already three days behind," Bhutta said.

"Let's get started!" Siddu added.

The mindset was locked in. Battle mode: ON.

"Sales Showdown: Gotya's Ego vs. Our Targets"

"Good morning," Siddu greeted, munching on an apple.

"Morning. Where's Bhutta?" I asked.

"Gotya called for him. Probably about some reports," Siddu replied, half an apple still in his mouth.

"Do you ever eat a proper breakfast?" I probed.

"Rujuta Aunty (the dietician) says apple first," Siddu said with all the wisdom of a health guru.

"Right. Let me see what's happening with Bhutta," I said, heading towards Gotya's cabin.

"Bhutta, I told you to send daily reports by evening. Why didn't I get yesterday's?" Gotya barked.

"May I come in?" I asked, sensing drama.

"Yes," Gautam reluctantly replied.

"What's going on?" I asked, acting clueless but wanting the full scoop.

"He hasn't sent yesterday's report," Gotya replied, still fuming.

"I told them to stop with daily reports and focus on weekly projections," I said calmly.

"Bhutta, you can go," Gotya dismissed him, then turned to me, his anger barely contained.

"Performance is down, and now you're canceling daily reports? Do you even know where this is heading?" Gotya was laying out consequences like a fortune teller at a carnival.

"We're heading toward better results. Trust me on this one. I'll explain the new projection sheet. If you've got time before lunch, I can show you. It's going to give us visibility on upcoming revenue," I said, letting my experience do the talking.

"But we never needed this before, and we still hit our numbers," Gotya grumbled, clearly stuck in the Stone Age.

"Let's try something new," I suggested firmly.

"Okay, I'll let you know when we can discuss it," he said, still skeptical.

I missed Venky today. Sure, he'd whine and ride us hard, but he'd always cover our backs with the higher-ups. Gotya? He was just out to feed his ego and throw us under the bus. No wonder salespeople kept leaving; his public insults were driving them away. If I didn't sort out his attitude with Bhutta and Siddu soon, I'd be the next course in his soup of incompetence.

I returned to my desk to find Siddu finishing his apple & gossiping with Kakubai (His gossip buddy).

"Did you bring lunch?" I asked.

"Yes, Boss," he replied, all proud.

"Well, starting today, we leave the office by 11 AM. Lunch? We'll figure that out on the road."

"But... what about my tiffin? Where do I eat?" Siddu, ever the routine follower, looked worried.

"Eat at a bus stop for all I care, just be out of the office by 11," I said. I knew it sounded harsh, but staying in the office wasn't going to help us hit our targets.

"Oh, and we'll return by 5 PM to plan for the next day. Meetings, schedules, everything," I added.

"But we already have a scrum meeting in the morning. Why do we need to come back?" Bhutta asked, his voice soft but curious.

"You'll understand with time," I said, standing firm. They nodded, trusting my madness had a method.

By 10:45 AM, Siddu and Bhutta had left. I was packing up when I heard a yell from behind.

"Where the hell are you going?" Gotya was standing outside his cabin, screaming loud enough for the entire floor to hear. They all ignored him, used to his tantrums.

It was the first time he'd spoken to me like that. I felt my face flush with anger, holding myself together.

"No one talks to me like that—not even my father. Next time, be careful," I said, loud enough for the entire floor to hear.

"I'm not your father! Where are the reports? And where are your missing jokers? Call them. I need my reports!" he bellowed.

"I'm heading to meetings. Reports come to me now—I'm their boss. I decide when and where they go. And as for my reports, you'll get them when I'm back," I shot back, keeping my cool.

"I'm your boss too! This is insubordination, and it could get you fired!" he threatened.

"If you're my boss, act like one. Meetings matter more than sending you reports.

Disagree? Go cry to your boss," I said. "You've already put my job on the line, so I don't care much about getting fired."

The floor went silent. For the first time, someone had given Gulya what he deserved.

"See you in the evening," I said with a wicked smile and walked out. I had nothing to lose.

Siddu and Bhutta were waiting downstairs near the tea-stall, expecting me early.

"Gotya was asking about reports," I said.

"What did you say?" Bhutta asked.

"Nothing. I'll manage him and his reports. You guys send everything to me, not him," I reminded them.

"What if he asks?" Siddu asked, always the cautious one.
"Tell him you sent it to me. I'll summarize and send it to him," I reassured.

"Did he check the projection sheet?" Bhutta asked.

"He didn't bother. Honestly, it's better that way. I'll send him the weekly report. The CEO understands it, and that's what matters. Gotya? He's useless," I said, shaking my head.

"Tea?" Bhutta asked.

"Yeah, and I need a cigarette too. Puff, puff—let's get back to work."

Chasing Sales, Sipping Tea, and a Bengali Beauty:
My First Month of Chaos

The client list was ready, neatly divided into three categories: The Loyals (the faithful print advertisers), PSUs (fans of print but allergic to digital), and the New Age private advertisers (who seemed to be advertising with everyone except us). Siddu got stuck chasing the PSUs, while Bhutta handled the mass advertisers. The bigger fish? Well, I kept those for myself, diving in from the very first meeting.

We had a daunting target of 35 Lakhs for the quarter—triple what we'd achieved last time. The first thing I did was hike up our card rates by 30% and made sure we didn't sell for anything less than 2 Lakhs per order. Then, I zeroed in on the five agencies that contributed 90% of the market's total orders. Siddu and Bhutta were assigned their parts, but I personally made sure to schmooze with every media planner from these top agencies, making sure we were on their radar.

His task? To constantly remind them we existed, even if it meant bribing them with tea breaks (coincidentally, of course). We had to make them feel our presence, even if it was just our faces popping up every few days. With Bhutta by my side, we smiled, waved, and—here's the fun part—added them to our Facebook friends list. From there, we liked and commented on most of their posts, turning ourselves into the perfect blend of colleagues and stalkers. By day 20, I swear we were in their inboxes, feeds, and probably even their dreams.

Things weren't all smooth, though. Siddu, poor guy, was frustrated after another long day at SBI Bank. "Boss, I'm done. Gupta (the Media Head) doesn't even look at me. Today, a young girl walks in, and suddenly he's offering her tea, chatting for 30 minutes, and promising her business. I've been sitting there for three months, and he still tells me to 'come tomorrow.' I'm never going back!"

I burst out laughing. "Siddu, relax! First of all, a sex change is a bit extreme, and I'm not sure Gupta's even worth it." Siddu didn't appreciate the joke, but I continued, "PSUs are slow, but they come through eventually. Tomorrow, go back with a smile, talk up your

SBI savings account, and mention how proud you are that your parents have worked for SBI. Trust me, you'll get tea and maybe even biscuits next time."

"But... I don't have an SBI account, and my parents never worked with SBI, they even hate their service!" Siddu groaned.

"Siddu, forget the emotions. Just stick to the plan. Here's a PPT—print it and treat that office like a temple. Someday, the gods will reward you."

I casually dropped the news that the print sales team had smashed their target and was celebrating with pizza—and, oh, by the way, two stunning Bengali girls had just joined them. Siddu's eyes lit up like a kid in a candy store. "Hold up, Bipasha lookalikes?" he asked, practically bouncing in his seat. You could see the gears turning in his head, his disappointment from the day instantly replaced with curiosity. Ah, Siddu—a little gossip was all it took to bring him back to life.

During the town hall, I finally saw Sohini for the first time—wow. Her almond-shaped eyes lined with kohl, sharp features, and dusky complexion were captivating. And her body? Voluptuous, with curves that made everyone in the room take notice. The other girl was just as striking, a perfect blend of Bengali and Assamese heritage. But it was Sohini who truly caught my eye. I hadn't felt this way in years, too buried in work to even notice anyone. Suddenly, I was all too aware.

The CEO gave a quick speech, showering the print team with praise while Siddu and Bhutta sulked. I kept my cool, knowing patience was our real challenge. But between the sales pressure and Sohini's unexpected arrival, staying focused became a whole new game.

By the end of the month, we had managed to pull in 5.5 lakhs, falling short by 29.5 Lakhs. I updated the CEO regularly—even once while we were both in the restroom, which was awkward but effective. He knew we were grinding and assured me that approvals wouldn't be a problem.

As I closed out the month, I realized two things: 1) We were nowhere near the target. 2) I was totally distracted by Sohini. Just what I needed—a crush at the worst possible time. "Stay focused, Dubey," I told myself. But that was easier said than done.

"Sales, Swagger, and Surprises: The Art of Staying in the Game"

In the second month, things were heating up both in sales and in the realm of romance. I made headway with a slew of high-profile clients: Vodafone, Raymonds, Asian Paints, Oracle Business, British Airways, ZOHO Corp, ICICI, and HDFC Bank. Proposals were flying out the door to Oracle, Vodafone, and ZOHO Corp, while HDFC and Asian Paints were still in the warm-up phase.

Bhutta and I doubled down on the big agencies—GroupM, Ogilvy, FCB Ulka, OMD, and Interactive Avenues—making almost daily pilgrimages to their offices. Siddu, on the other hand, got a tiny victory when Gupta from SBI Bank requested a copy of our presentation, though Gupta himself remained a no-show. Siddu also discovered that Bank of India hadn't even ventured into digital advertising yet, proving once again that temples, like sales, require patience.

One day, while having lunch at Royal Lunch Home with Girish, he gave me a nudge and said, "Hey, your darling is sitting two tables away from us, behind you." I turned around and, sure enough, there was Sohini with her friend Indrani. My heart skipped a beat. Girish winked at me, and they laughed. I couldn't help but wonder why women find nervousness so amusing.

Girish then asked, "Shall I get you introduced?"

"Seriously, you talk to them?" I replied, though my excitement was barely contained. "Yeah, sure, I'd love that!"

"Come with me," Girish said, and we joined their table. I was a bundle of nerves. My heart raced, and I tried to steady my breath.

Girish introduced me with a grin. "This is Dubey, my friend who works in Sales. He's pretty good at what he does. We usually eat here, and it's nice to see you both!"

They greeted me, and I managed to return the pleasantries. But honestly, I was mesmerized. Sohini's beauty was stunning—whether it was her natural allure or my crush amplifying it, I couldn't say.

Sohini broke the silence with, "So, you're always this quiet?"

Girish chuckled and added, "He talks a lot, I guess he's just quiet because he's seeing you."

I blushed and replied, "No, I'm not quiet. I'm just a little introverted."

Indrani, with a playful smile, asked, "What are you doing in sales then?" The three of them laughed, and I found myself smiling, though I wasn't quite sure what to say next.

After lunch, Girish said to me, "You better focus on sales. She doesn't look achievable. You're too shy!"

I took the challenge and responded, "Bet."

Girish raised the stakes. "Okay, if you can get her attention within one month, I'll treat you to dinner at a restaurant of your choice and a bottle of scotch."

"Bet for two months," I countered.

"Alright," Girish said, "and if you can't, you're sponsoring a trip for me and yourself to a place of my choice. And I'll still take that bottle of scotch."

"Deal," I agreed.

Meanwhile, Bhutta and I had a meeting with Vodafone. We met with Amar, the GM Marketing, who was a very professional guy. I took notes on what he wanted for the upcoming marketing campaign and asked about the budget. He said, "You can suggest something, but make sure to meet our agency, GroupM."

Later that day, we also met Raymonds, where the traditional marketing guy Ganesh was open to innovative ideas and requested a proposal. I noted everything, and we went back to prepare the minutes of the meeting and shared them via email. I set a turnaround time of four days to respond with proposals for both clients.

However, 15 days went by without any new orders. We kept sending proposals and meeting with potential clients, though securing meetings remained a challenge at times. I gave the sales team strict instructions to stick to the sales pitch, and as a result, our success rate in scheduling meetings improved with each call for an appointment.

I prepared and sent proposals to Raymonds and Vodafone, and we met with their respective agencies, GroupM and RK Swamy. Bhutta managed to secure one more RO from Interactive Avenues. We closed a deal with Axis Bank for 3.5 Lacs over a delivery period of 45 days, which I helped seal. Despite these wins, we were 9 Lacs short - Our target was 35 Lacs with 40 days remaining, and the pressure was mounting.

I started visiting Girish more often, but let's be real—everyone knew I was really there to see Sohini. I'd say, "Hi, Girish," but my eyes were always on her, and she'd flash that smile, responding with a sweet "Hello."

It didn't take long for everyone to figure it out. My "work" visits were just a cover-up. The real deal was trying to impress Sohini, and I was pulling out all the stops. Luckily, I've got a knack for cracking jokes. Every time I popped by, I'd throw in a funny line or two, and the whole room would laugh. But Sohini? She always laughed the loudest.

One day, I spotted Sohini heading toward the pantry and thought, "Perfect opportunity." I casually strolled up and said, "Hey, Sohini, I need a favor. I've decided to learn Bengali. You know, just in case it helps me impress a certain someone."

With a grin, she said, "Oh, sure! We can speak Bengali whenever we bump into each other. I'd be more than happy to help you charm that SOMEONE."

I'm pretty sure the sarcasm in her tone could be felt in two different languages.

I took a deep breath and said, "Kemun Achen (How are you?)"

She replied with a smile, "Bhalo (I'm good)."

"Abar dekha hobe (See you again)," I chuckled, and Sohini laughed. We started talking more, and I felt a genuine connection.

The Pitch That Almost Wasn't: Turning Setbacks into Comebacks

One afternoon, Butta called me with concern. "Boss, this media planner for Vodafone is being difficult. He said you should have informed him about meeting the client directly. We don't appreciate publishers meeting our clients without notice."

I asked, "What's the status?"

He replied, "He's not sure if he'll give us any order. All the budgets are already planned."

"Alright," I said, "fix a meeting with David tomorrow. I'll meet with a Vodafone client."

"Okay, Boss," Bhutta responded.

I then called Siddu, "What's the progress with Bank of India, SBI, and Union Bank?"

"They're cold, Boss," Siddu replied.

"Okay," I instructed, "fix meetings with them. I'll come along. It's time to change gears."

"Understood, Boss," Siddu confirmed.

The next day, we went to meet David—a junior planner for Vodafone working with a top media agency. He was the kind of guy whose arrogance could fill a room. Overconfident and smug, David already decided he wasn't including us in the media plan without even reading our proposal.

"Have you had a chance to look at our proposition?" I asked.

He shrugged, "No. But we're not going with you guys."

Just like that, no reading, no consideration. We had prepared a detailed 15-slide PPT offering a sponsorship package worth ₹12 lakhs. The inventory alone was valued at over ₹15 lakhs in the market, and we promised excellent performance and audience engagement. The deck included cutting-edge innovations that no website had ever done before. We even mocked up how it would look on their platform. It was impressive, to say the least.

I kept my cool and said, "David, it's alright if you feel there's no space for us in the media plan, but at least take a look at what we've prepared. You're free to steal these ideas and pitch them to your other clients."

I had also invited Manjunath, David's boss, to the meeting. I sent him the PPT and knew he might join at any moment. The moment David heard that his boss might join, his arrogance took a back seat, and he agreed to listen.

Five minutes later, Manjunath walked in. Both of them were impressed with our pitch, but they still weren't budging. "The client's already frozen the plan," they said.

As we walked out of the office, Bhutta looked downcast. "What now, Boss? We worked so hard for this, wasted a whole month, and David just screwed us."

I dialed Amar, our contact at Vodafone. "Hi Amar, how's it going?"

"Doing great, man. What's up?"

"Listen, could you spare 10 minutes for a quick meet sometime this week?"

"Sure. How about in three days?"

"Perfect! See you then." I hung up and turned to Bhutta with a grin.

"Bhutta," I said, "we never waste time in sales. We invest it. We've got a meeting with Amar in three days. We're still in the game."

He brightened up. "So, what's the plan?"

"We keep playing, my friend. Always."

"Deadline Drama: Deals, Dates, and a Dash of Romance"

We were in the third month of the quarter with just 30 days left, and the pressure to close deals was insane. Siddu was feeling the heat the most, sitting on nothing but promises from his PSU clients. He had been hustling like crazy, following up relentlessly. Most of them were friendly by now, even Gupta, who smiled and offered him tea but still didn't give him an official meeting.

Siddu and Bhutta each had a target of 10 lacs, which would help us reach 20 lacs. I had taken on 15 lacs but was pushing for 20 or more, just to blow past our goals. But honestly, at that point, it felt impossible. And there was Gotya, all smiles during the weekly meetings, while everyone silently questioned my ability to deliver. Hell, sometimes even I doubted myself. But then I'd tell myself, "Trust the process."

During the next weekly meeting, the CEO called me in. Gotya was sitting in the corner, as usual, with that smug grin on his face. The CEO looked me dead in the eyes and said, "We've got 15 days left, technically 11 if you take out the weekends. I don't see this happening."

Gotya, still grinning, added, "Time to call movers and packers! We'll need your desk for someone else soon!" He laughed, relishing the moment.

I stayed calm. "Sir, we'll get it done. I trust my boys, their hard work, and mine too."

Gotya interrupted, "Hard work doesn't pay bills."

The CEO shot back, "You stick to your promise, I'll stick to mine. Simple."

"Yes, sir," I said, walking out of the room. As soon as I hit the washroom, I splashed water on my face. A tear slipped out, and I whispered to myself, "Trust the process."

As I walked back, I bumped into Sohini. She smiled and said, "Hello." I just gave a nod, trying not to show the storm inside. Lately, we'd been talking a lot—two or three hours every night, like good friends, but I knew it was more. We'd met a couple of times outside work too—once at Worli Sea Face and another time to pay tribute to the 26/11 martyrs. We were planning a coffee date soon.

Even Girish teased me, saying I didn't have the guts to confess my feelings. Maybe he was right. I was dropping hints but never making a move. Heck, I was even learning Bengali because of her—I could string together a few sentences with the right accent now!

Later that day, Sohini called. "Everything okay?" she asked, her voice full of concern.

I wanted to tell her, "No, nothing's okay," but I couldn't bring myself to say it. Maybe I was afraid of looking weak. It's hard to understand why, in our society, a man showing his emotions is often seen as a weakness. It's ingrained in us so deeply, and I've never quite understood why.

"Yeah, just a rough sales day," I brushed it off. We talked for 15 minutes before hanging up. She gave me space, sensing something wasn't quite right.

The next two days were a whirlwind of client meetings. Bhutta kept chasing David, who kept giving him the same old line, "I'll get back to you." I reached out to Amar at Vodafone, and after two days, we finally met. "Did they not give you the PO (Purchase Order) yet?" Amar asked, surprised.

"No, not yet."

Amar immediately called David. "I asked you to give them 8 lacs. What's the holdup? No, this campaign. Not the next one. Okay? Good."

Bhutta, standing nearby, grinned like a baby elephant. "Boss, let's celebrate today!"

"Not yet," I cautioned. "No PO in the email, no celebration. But keep at it."

That evening, Sohini called and said, "I've booked us a place after work. I'm buying you coffee."

"Okay, what time?" I asked, feeling lighter already.

"8 PM, Phoenix Mall. Don't be late."

I hung up, and Bhutta, as usual, smirked at me. "What?" I asked, narrowing my eyes.

"Nothing," he chuckled, walking away.

Meanwhile, I had pitched a similar deal to Raymond for 10 lakhs and was waiting for a reply. Siddu was still sitting at zero. It's been two days of following up with Raymond, and there's still no response.

That evening, around 6:30 PM, just as I was getting ready for my coffee date, I got a call from an unknown number. "Hi, this is Ganesh."

"Ganesh from Raymond?" I asked, straightening up.

"Yeah, listen, we can't do 10 lacs. How about 6? Digital is new to us."

"Ganesh, come on, let's sweeten the deal. You've been a loyal client for a long time, and you know we always come through. Trust me, I won't let you down."

"How much are you suggesting?" he asked, hesitant.

"Let's do 8 lacs."

"Alright, RK Swamy will send you a PO for 8 lacs. Email okay?"

"Of course!" I hung up and looked up at the sky, whispering, "Thank you!"

I called Bhutta and Siddu. They were thrilled. But we still needed 21 lacs to hit our target.

I reached on time, and there she was, waiting near Starbucks. Her face practically glowed in the evening light. She wore a white kurti with blue jeans, her hair cascading down in waves, and I couldn't help but notice just how sexy she looked—effortlessly stunning, yet with a quiet elegance that made it impossible to look away. The way her kurti hugged her figure had my mind wandering in ways it probably shouldn't have, but hey, I'm only human, right?

I walked up to her, feeling a mix of excitement and nervousness. "Shall we?" I asked, trying to keep my cool.

She smiled, her eyes catching mine in that way that sent a spark through me. "Someone's actually on time," she teased, raising an eyebrow. "I like that."

Later that night, over coffee, I asked Sohini, "Do you drink alcohol?"

"I drink wine only on special occasions," she smiled. "And you?"

"Almost on every occasion," I joked.

As we walked back after our coffee date, I casually held her hand while crossing the road, and for some reason, I just didn't let go. Her hands were warm, and she had this soft smile on her face. She never asked me to let go, so we kept walking, hand in hand, for what felt like forever. It was awesome—I couldn't stop talking.

I opened up about the mess we were dealing with at the office, how Gotya was making life unbearable, and how the team was struggling to hit targets, all while dealing with office politics. She listened quietly the entire time, no interruptions, just understanding. We must've walked for over an hour by now, and I could feel she genuinely cared about what I was going through.

As we neared her place, she finally spoke. "It's getting late," she said, glancing at her watch. "I think I'll take a taxi from here."

"Mind if I tag along and take the same taxi back home?"

She smiled, eyes widening just a little, and nodded. When we reached her stop, she gave me a hug and placed her hand gently on my cheek. "You're honest and hardworking," she said softly. "Things will fall into place. Good night!"

And just like that, the world felt a little lighter.

The next morning, I woke up to an email in my inbox—it was the PO from RKSwamy! Ganesh had honored his promise of 10 lakhs. I immediately forwarded it to Gotya, with the CEO and ops team CC'd. Moments later, the CEO replied, "Congrats! This is just the beginning—more to come!"

By the afternoon, Bhutta and I bagged another 4 lacs from Toyota. **We were at 50% of our target but still needed 17 lacs.**

I called David and Manjunath again—still nothing. With just three days left in the month, things weren't looking good. I checked my watch. It was 3 PM. I texted Amar, "Hey, quick smoke break? I'm nearby." He replied, "No chance, buddy. Drowning in work, maybe next time."

I almost typed back, "What about the PO you promised?" but decided to hold back. No point being overly aggressive, I reminded myself.

Then, at 6 PM, David finally emailed me. "Hi, apologies for the delay. I was waiting for internal approvals. Attached PO: 9 lakhs." I knew for sure Amar must've shoved his magic wand up David's ass to make this happen.

Bhutta called me, practically bursting with excitement, "Boss, we're almost there! And can you believe David actually said sorry? I'm shocked!"

"Not a word to anyone yet," I warned. "Get it printed, stamped by GroupM, and keep the hard copy with you."

Later, Amar texted, "1 lakh extra for the trouble. Might change agencies soon—they're not professionals."

"Just 8 lacs more," I reminded myself. **Deep down, I knew our jobs were safe, but this wasn't just about hitting targets anymore. I wanted to make a statement—to Gotya, to the CEO, and to myself**. It was about proving we were more than just numbers on a spreadsheet. I could feel the pressure, but instead of fear, it fueled my determination. **Now, it was personal. I wasn't just closing deals; I was setting the record straight.**

We planned to hit the field hard the next day. That night, I messaged Sohini on WhatsApp, "I love you," but quickly deleted it. She asked, "What did you delete?"

"Nothing important," I replied, smiling to myself.

The judgment day - Month End - 30th

The next morning, we hit the ground running. Gotya messaged, "No one's in the office today—perfect time for movie breaks! Don't forget your promise to the CEO. Good luck!" Little did he know, we were just 8 lakhs short of the target.

I ignored his message like a fart in the wind.

Bhutta went agency-hopping, I chased clients for any last-minute deals, and Siddu? Still sitting on zero. I thought about giving him a share of my business, but I knew even one lakh short, and we'd be in deep trouble.

Sohini called me, sounding all concerned. "Hey, everything okay?"

"Yeah, so far so good," I replied. "But honestly, I don't think we're gonna make it. I've had six meetings already, dialed all the follow-ups since morning, and still... nothing."

"Cheer up, handsome! Things will fall into place. You guys are rock solid as a team, just keep grinding," she said, trying to boost my spirits.

Then, the big question: "What did you have for lunch?"

"Vada pav and tea," I answered casually.

"Vada pav? It's 3 PM and that's all you've had? Get yourself a Subway or something. Hunger will steal your wisdom!"

"Yeah, yeah, I'll see," I muttered, not really paying attention. "Anyway, I gotta run, heading into my 7th meeting of the day."

I was at Bank of India, yet another client that had promised Siddu some business. We'd already submitted a 6-lakh proposal, and they'd given a verbal confirmation. But honestly, this was Bank of India—a place that had never done digital ads before. Why would they start now? Even if we landed the 6 lakhs, we'd still be 2 lakhs short of the target. My CEO's voice echoed in my head like the devil whispering, "You keep your promise, and I'll keep mine."

Great, I thought. Even if we're short by 10k, we're dead.

I walked into the meeting with the GM, and he hit me with, "Mr. Dubey, we're still waiting for approvals from Head Office. It's not in yet, but I promise you'll get the business I committed to. Could be today, could be in 2-3 days. If it comes through today, I'll give it to you today. You're welcome to wait until 6 PM."

"Sir, it's month-end. It would mean the world to us if we got it today," I replied, holding on to whatever hope I had left.

So, I sat in the lounge with no choice but to wait. This was my last shot for the day. While waiting, I started making follow-up calls to clear my list.

At 5 PM, Gotya messaged, "No calls since morning. Clock's ticking, Mr. Dubey."

"Asshole," I muttered to myself. I wished I could send that reply to him directly, but that would end everything in a heartbeat.

By 5:30 PM, Bhutta was done for the day, he had no luck either. I asked him to call one more time for follow ups, we may get lucky.

I was about to call Siddu when he rang me up, shouting, "I got it! I got the PO!"

"Who gave it? How much?" I asked, stunned.

"Gupta gave 10 lacs. 10 freaking lacs!" he was practically dancing on the phone.

"Is it signed and stamped?"

"Yes!"

We met near Phoenix Mall, and I double-checked the order—completely legit. Siddu, beaming like a kid who just aced his first spelling bee, said, "So, I sat there while he flirted with the girls. Then, as he was heading out, he casually goes, 'You're persistent. Here's your PO. Had it ready before you even walked in—I knew, just like clockwork, you'd show up.'"

The man practically gave Siddu a medal for being a professional stalker!

Gotya texted, "Any orders, Sir?"—clearly hoping we'd crashed and burned like he predicted.

I shot back, "Check your inbox. **SIR**."

I called the CEO. "Sir, we've done 37 lacs against the target of 35 lacs."

"Congratulations! Plan for Goa. I'll join you guys. Well done."

I called Sohini, excitement bubbling in my voice. "We did it! We overachieved our targets. We're partying tonight!"

She laughed, "Hahaha, congrats, Dubeyji! I'm proud of you and your boys. Make sure to drink one beer for me!"

Without thinking, I blurted, "One more thing—I love you."

I hung up, stunned by my own words. Did I really just say that? I'm not shy; I'm in love.

That night, we partied like there was no tomorrow. We hit 37 lacs, smashing our target of 35 lacs. Almost teary-eyed, I looked up and whispered, "Thank you, God!"

And we celebrate....GOA here we come

Three days later, we found ourselves in Goa. Gotya, true to form, bailed with some lame health excuse. The CEO popped in for a quick visit, but it was us, the team, savoring the sweet taste of victory. We arrived in the afternoon, freshened up, and geared up for a wild night of celebration. By 2 AM, we were completely toasted, staggering back to our rooms, laughing like kids.

As I collapsed on the bed, my phone buzzed. I'd missed a few calls from Sohini. Her message flashed on the screen: *"Hey, I wanted to say something."*

Grinning, I replied, *"Yeah, say it."*

Her reply was swift: *"Call me."*

I didn't waste a second. Dialed her up immediately. She whispered on the other end, "I love you too. Propose to me properly when you're back. I want to see your eyes when you say it. Good night, love!"

Bhutta, the nosy one, had been peeking over my shoulder the whole time. He smirked, "So, what now, Boss?"

With a dramatic flourish, I pulled out my Cuban cigar like a mafia don. "This, my friend, is made in Cuba. And now, we have a tribal dance to perform!"

"Tribal dance?" Bhutta raised an eyebrow, totally confused.

I nodded like I knew some ancient secret. "The brotherhood… of keeping secrets!"

"Grab your bedsheets from the room," I commanded, channeling my inner general. "Siddu, go find some strong sticks—preferably the kind that won't snap under pressure, unlike our sales targets!"

Both burst out laughing, shaking their heads. "Whatever you say, Boss!"

About the Author

Deepak Dubey

Deepak Dubey, an MBA in Marketing from Mumbai University, brings 18 years of experience in Sales & Marketing. With deep expertise in media and enterprise sales, he has successfully led large teams, focusing on solution selling and client management. His specialization in digital sales, SEO, social media, and digital marketing, along with founding two successful ventures, highlights his entrepreneurial edge.

In *Street Smarts - How Life's Hustlers Taught Me to Sell*, Deepak combines his vast sales knowledge with humor, offering readers practical insights and entertaining stories from the corporate world.

Thank you!

Hola,

Thank you for embarking on this journey with me through *Street Smarts*. Your support and enthusiasm mean the world to me. I hope you enjoyed the candid look at the sales world and found the stories both entertaining and insightful.

I'm grateful for your interest and am excited to let you know that this is just the beginning. You can expect more books from me in the future, each bringing new stories and adventures.

Thank you once again for your encouragement and for being part of this journey. Stay tuned for what's next!

Warm regards,

Deepak Dubey